nickelodeon

DORA the EXPLORER

Dora and the Winter Games

By Martha T. Ottersley
Illustrated by Susan Hall

A Random House PICTUREBACK® Book

Random House 🏠 New York

ISBN 978-0-385-37930-4
randomhouse.com/kids
Printed in the United States of America
10 9 8 7 6 5 4 3 2

Dora and Boots were so excited! It was time for
the Winter Games, held high atop Snowy Mountain.
   "I can't wait to see all the animals race!" said Dora.
   "Me too!" agreed Boots.

The racers took their places at the starting line. "Look, look!" cheered Boots. "There's Swifty the polar bear. He is the fastest skier."

"*Mira*," said Dora. "There's Slider the penguin! He will be the best at sledding."

"And there's Hoppy. She loves skating!" said Boots.
"This is going to be an exciting race!"

Suddenly, a loud voice announced, "It's time for the winter games to begin!" The crowd grew very quiet. "Racers—on your marks, get set, GO!" And they were off!

But just as the race began, an owl flew down in a fluttery fluster.

"Help, help! There's a problem with the race course!" he panted. "The Ice Bridge at the end of the trail is broken! The racers won't be able to cross it and reach the finish line. Whoo—whoo—WHO can help?"

"Boots and I can help!" shouted Dora. "If we get to the Ice Bridge before the racers, we can fix it so they can cross."

"But how will we get there first?" asked Boots. "The racers are all so fast!"

"We need to find the quickest way to the Ice Bridge," said Dora. "Who do we ask for help when we don't know which way to go?"

Dora and Boots called for their friend Map.

Map told them that they had to ski down the Black Diamond Trail, then skate across Slippery Pond, and finally sled down the Steepest Slope.

"*Gracias, Map,*" said Dora.

Dora and Boots put on their skis and helmets before zooming off to the Black Diamond Trail. They saw other shapes, but they found the right trail.

Dora and Boots were so fast that they skied right past Swifty! "The Ice Bridge is broken!" Dora called. "We're trying to get there first so we can fix it."

Swifty waved a big paw. "Now we need to keep going to Slippery Pond!" said Dora.

At Slippery Pond, they saw a row of skates. *"¡Rápido!"* said Dora. "We can use these ice skates to cross Slippery Pond!"
But just as they were reaching for the skates, they heard a rustling sound nearby.

Dora and Boots turned around and saw Swiper sneaking up on them.

"That sneaky fox will try to swipe our skates!" Dora said. "Swiper, no swiping!"

"Oh, mannn!" said Swiper as he snapped his fingers and ran away.

Dora and Boots put on their skates. "Now we can skate across the pond," Dora said. "Let's hurry! *¡Vámonos!*"
Dora and Boots set off across the ice as fast as they could.

Dora and Boots skated faster and faster. Suddenly, they saw some trees that had fallen on the ice. "Get ready, Boots!" shouted Dora. "We have to jump!"

"How many times do we need to jump?" asked Boots.
"Let's count!" answered Dora. "¡Uno, dos, tres, cuatro, cinco!"
"Five! We have to jump five times!" said Boots.

Dora and Boots jumped over the five trees and zipped straight past Hoppy!

"The Ice Bridge is broken," Dora told her. "We're trying to get there to fix it!"

"Hop to it!" said Hoppy. She gave them a thumbs-up.

Dora and Boots swapped their skates for a sled and rocketed down the Steepest Slope so fast, they passed Slider the penguin!

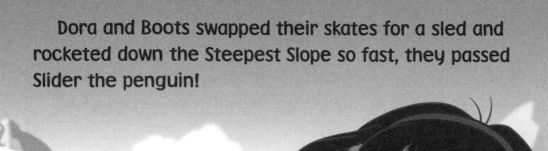

"The Ice Bridge is broken," Dora called to Slider. "We're trying to get there first so we can fix it!"

Slider gave them a big smile.

Dora and Boots reached the bottom of the Steepest Slope and ran to the broken Ice Bridge.

"The bridge is missing four icy pieces!" said Dora. "To fix the bridge, we need to figure out which pieces fit in the spaces."

"Let's look at the gaps," said Dora. "There are four gaps, and they are all shaped like rectangles. We need to find those pieces!"

Together, Dora and Boots found the missing pieces and put them back into the Ice Bridge.

Just then, Slider, Hoppy, and Swifty sped over the Ice
Bridge and crossed the finish line at exactly the same time!
"We did it! *iLo hicimos!*" Dora cheered as Boots clapped.
"But whoo—whoo—WHO is the winner of the Winter
Games?" asked the owl.

The racers huddled together for a moment.
"We all agree that the winners should be whoever
was the best at skiing, skating, and sledding," said Swifty.

"And most importantly, we couldn't have had the
Winter Games without them," said Hoppy.
"The winners of this year's Winter Games are . . ."

"Dora and Boots!"

Everyone clinked their mugs of hot chocolate in celebration!